CW01216861

WEATHER DERIVATIVES

RUFO QUINTAVALLE

WEATHER DERIVATIVES

☐☐ **EYEWEAR** PUBLISHING

First published in 2014
by Eyewear Publishing Ltd
74 Leith Mansions, Grantully Road
London W9 1LJ
United Kingdom

Typeset with graphic design by Edwin Smet
Author photograph Renaud Monfourny
Printed in England by TJ International Ltd, Padstow, Cornwall

All rights reserved
© 2014 Rufo Quintavalle

The right of Rufo Quintavalle to be identified as author of
this work has been asserted in accordance with section 77
of the Copyright, Designs and Patents Act 1988
ISBN 978-1-908998-37-8

WWW.EYEWEARPUBLISHING.COM

Rufo Quintavalle
was born in London in 1978,
studied at Oxford and the
University of Iowa and lives in
Paris where he is active in the
field of environmental impact
investing. He is the author
of several chapbooks
the most recent of which,
*moral hazard and the
chemical sweats*, was
published by corrupt press
in 2013. He was formerly
poetry editor for the
award-winning webzine
Nthposition and served on
the editorial board for the
Paris-based literary journal
Upstairs at Duroc. He is
currently working on a
collaborative work
with the British composer
James Weeks.

Table of Contents

A week, a year, whatever — 9
You and whose army — 15
Transatlantic rift — 16
Place du Carrousel — 17
teeth shook and jasmine — 18
Invisible hand job — 20
Filling — 21
Drunken bride — 22
A day at the zoo — 25
Brutus — 26
Last year's man — 27
The country — 28
Names and the animals — 29
Dumbo — 30
Home again — 31
Because the night — 32
Rocks — 34
How it ends — 35
Two for one — 36
I admire — 37
sunday — 39
Cathedral — 40
there were all these birds — 41
Nowhere special — 44
2007 — 46
Letter from Iceland — 47
The point of pain — 49
I went down in the basement — 50
Static — 51
Ariel out of synch with the sun — 52

Stately — 53
Ball bearings — 54
Theories of Justice — 55
Well, here I am — 56
by the sea — 58
by the sea — 59
by the sea — 60
by the sea — 61
Miłosz in California — 62
May — 63
Much — 64
More — 66
Figs — 69

Acknowledgements — 71

A week, a year, whatever

i.

So many
        have
started

out from silence
but I will start
        from
something else

        like

maybe the sprawl
of this afternoon.

ii.

After all
        it really
has everything
        in it:

a tree, some noise
of cars

and not
        so long ago
lunch.

iii.

For the longest time

I worried
           people
would come
           up over

the wall
           and
get me
           but I don't

worry about that

anymore

even as I speak

a column of silica
is blowing over
Europe
           and all that
seems to matter
                are
the cancelled flights

I'm not even sure
this goal
           getting
the point

        of view

which would be
truly
        detached
from
        our own

self-interest
            is
desirable
        but still
from time
        to time

I wish we'd try

always to deny

the angelic
            in
our nature
        seems
to be
    the only role

someone decided
to leave the poets

well
        whoever they
were

   I never met
them
  and their dicta

carry small weight
with me

no, I think
    the wall
will hold
    just fine
and if
   it doesn't

let them
   come.

iv.

In the street
    it is

time for
   the children

to be picked up
from school
    they
will all go
   home
or more

   likely

(it is sunny
    today

like it hasn't
    been
in weeks)

    to a park

but one of the
    boys
is crying.

v.

This funny thing

happened
    then
I went
  up
    on
the roof
   and a
strong wind
picked up
   just as

the restaurant

switched off
              their
extractor fan

so one sound
stopped
        when
the other
         began

and the wind

carried off
the cooking smells

and

    tossed them
with
    the cumulus.

vi.

So you see, there really is everything.

You and whose army

A river drove and that was rot;
if that than which then I,
up early and seeking exposure
to the following themes, began:
the water, the water, the water to shave,
the water that, in drips, gives life,
in floods and gullies takes away;
the rank demographics, the road map of fear
and a spider, breathing, on Maghrebin tiles.

These are our best times, don't be fooled;
the best, that is, we'll ever know,
here on our ice cap,
here on our shrinking island,
starting, slant-eyed, out from next to nothing.
Remember when we drank wine?
That bottle so rich it filled like fisting
or an egg an egg our mouths?
I've a magnum hid in the children's playpen,
call up your friend, the one with the legs
and the sad eyes and we'll share it.

You and whose army says the boatman and I'm scared
but open like a gaping birth to anyone.

Transatlantic rift

Every year that is minutely every day Thingvellir
widens like law or the Tao change incrementally
this space where law is enacted grows.
It seems the natural thing to listen
whilst the Europeans talk the contrary habit
talking whilst the Europeans listen we have not
yet acquired, said Will iam James in Scotland.
Well, water has flown under the bridge since
now both sides chatter freely, neither hearing
the other or even making sense: a rose is a rose
by any other name. All the time the ground
moves underneath them as it should, a rift
the thing there is that doesn't love a wall.

We like our maps Euclidean, sugar
sweet but thicken lines and borders
swell to borderlands living space
like the stone furrow the Althing
met in to law talk, canyons
life rises from plankton mist
overflowing oceanic vents
the grooves of vinyl records or a brain
whose troughs are the lacunae
the line breaks of mind: sleep
fainting, coma epilepsy, the fact
of interruption being admitted, if only
by William James again, is it not possible
that it may exist in in cessant fine-grained form?
If so I am minded to do that drug or yoga
that will excavate a forgetting big
enough for parliament for beasts to graze in
redirect the stream so water fills the long
ravine and wait Idealists would plug
the gaps in sluggish Circady, concrete
rucked fields to smooth abstractions, but
being hominids origin gorge
this crack down the globe becomes us.

Place du Carrousel

The president passes in a motorcade;
let him pass.

The sun is kissing my eyes
and I know I shall never go hungry.

teeth shook and jasmine

my teeth shook   in
my skull   and jasmine
edged   distantly
it was far   and away
the best   we'd known
it   incomparable
afternoon   within a
mediocre year   you
suggested   a picnic
I   stripped off
there & then   celadon
sky   and similar sea
and so much   summer
to get   ourselves into
cars   like vultures
circling   like
no tomorrow   as if
no   not   like that
tutors   rather
the learning   curve
or the way   a runner
bean   turns   to grip
and matte paint   on
sun-ladened   walls
while   everywhere
else is   elsewhere
music of   intimate
and   anecdotal
life   stuff   she
screamed   and

screamed   and
no one came   the
day   advanced
towards its   horrible
end   and anodyne
matter   meant more
and more   honey
suckle   leaves
yellow   and fall
and a tongue   thick
from menthols   dabs
at   dry   lips

Invisible hand job

If love of money is the root of all evil,
could spending it be a source of good?
This ten-year potlatch not a crazy waste
but a vast, half-conscious benevolence;
to spend and never count the cost, buy
and ask for no reward, money flowing
through us like spunk through swingers.
You think you are fine with your ethics,
your thrift and sustainable investments?
I tell you the merest of clubbers is finer;
knickers in handbag, head splitting, spent.

Filling

Variations on emptiness
clutter my mind, a clot of thought,
of bubble wrap,
frogspawn.

It seems the story of the man
whose jaw like a sphincter closed around a pool ball
is a lie but I want to believe it,
plenitude, true.

Drunken bride

I had tried so many different things,
tried everything
but the fire wouldn't take;

the Christmas tree I had hacked to pieces
on the 6th of January in my 33rd year
then left for a month
to dry, sap forming beads
on the branches' cut ends
(crown of studs
around a breast)
was fed into the chimney
as kindling;
               the oil
in its needles fizzed
                           and the flames
reached up and round
the bought logs from the hardware store
and smelt as though the Seneca were blessing me with sage,
and died;

a friend said it was to do
with air: air
that needs to circulate
freely for fire
to burn,
       so I propped
the logs on other logs
                           right-angled
to give them height

and the air space,
>	like the sky
which Hopkins
>	held his hand
up into
>	and saw the mother of God in,
to move around in and		make
>	in moving
but the coals and twigs,
>	the little wood
burnt red hot and brilliant
>	and the big wood
wouldn't take.

I tried toxic stuff:
>	wrapping paper,
>	>	paper bags,
>	>	>	chopsticks,
>	>	>	>	detritus,
turned my living room to landfill,
billows spilling out and upwards,
>	>	staining
the artwork, shortening our lives;

I asked professional advice and learnt
that the very manufacture
of the fireplace		might be at fault,
that it might be too high for its width or depth
or any other of those two by three equations;
something,				warmed to this idea
>	the architect in (the poet in) me,

and like chess I experimented,
                          logs back
               middle
                               and forth
hung flaps of cardboard
                      from the mantel
piece's lip; surelevated the whole show
on a grill, as if if one could get the setting right,
the rest,
     like modernist Utopias
  or a barrow boy in a Savile Row suit
  would all just   fall into place.

   I tried other woods, I blew and fanned,
  I opened doors and windows and froze,
 the goal of warmth forgotten in the quest:
to make at least a small place work,
  and a void consume indefinitely

    but it wouldn't take,
    no matter what,

    & the skinny flame
    flickered
    like a
    drunken
    bride.

A day at the zoo

A rhesus macaque
aligns then mounts
a rhesus macaque

machines for existing

not even, parts
of a machine.

A rhino butts
a rock, stumbles.

We have nothing
in common
with the beasts.

If they could think,
or choose,
or starve themselves,
or parse their sex drives
into a thousand internally consistent flavours
each with a slew
of bars and websites,
if they, as well
as offspring,
made of
the presence of death,
codicils and worship,
would they

be of the same mind?

Brutus

We overslept and missed the spring again,
and then came an angry man,
spluttering blood, farting beluga.

Go away we said *with your mischief
and your hideous beard* but he stayed.

He scared my cousin with his talk of girls,
and my wife with his knowledge of money.
He put the fear of God in us all
and stayed forever: a hulking,
unwanted, necessary saint.

Last year's man

He and his car
each weighed a ton;
they were one
and the same,

dependent like a tree
grown round
a bench.

When he farted
Lindy farted too.

His morning breath
filled Lindy;
she was his blanket,
his special place.

Together they explored the world
and killed the plants and children.

The country

If I moved to the country
I would hear more birds,
eat less ethnic food
and see fewer crazies
covered in piss and faeces in the metro

but I cannot move to the country;
fifty percent of the world is here
sucking on the petrochemical tit
and until that changes
my place is among them.

Names and the animals

      Some poets know the names
    of almost all the animals
and what they do
      is they deploy them
not all at once
       but a smattering
  to bring the animals
     into focus
and make them
    enter their poems

 but all I hear
      is man, is me
and it isn't the animals
   come but language;

the tug of barbed
      wire or an abattoir's
     heavy plastic
  flap is where
     the animals rub
 against our world
   like strangers
 in the tube
     like messengers
     not names.

Dumbo

The elephant's ears are angelic wings
that spank the wicked, caress the good
and lull the young, who are neithernor, to sleep.
Egyptians used ears to mummy their dead,
the Greeks to win shade in immaculate stoas.
4:15, sometime in November, a plane pierces
the rainy night like a needle through the lobe
of an elephant's ear; in summer they bat
like ricepaper kites, wafting traffic, birdsong,
the works across the soft agnostic weather.

Home again

I'm home again, combing out my long hair
while the rooks do their number,
yammering away like klaxons,
wreaking havoc with the domestics' nerves.
You'd think you'd get used to it but you don't.

Before the windfall I worked on a train,
oiling the central piston.
I never clocked on or off, just woke, oiled, ate, then slept
while the train went steadily forwards.
Sometimes I oiled till it shone in the night
like a terrible ebony god.

It was easy work but I quit. Because of the windfall.
Now I stay home nights and most days too,
combing my hair, planning.
I do my best to calm the staff
but if truth be told I'm scared;
it seems the train runs fine without me
and behind the birds I can hear the sluice
of that dark redundant piston.

Because the night

Because the night
surrounds us,
because the cold
has got up
through our feet,
because the street
curves gently,
because in the dark
neon and an odor
of felt, because
the cellar door,
because the night,
despite the heart's
imperative, thins,
because the distant
sky the stairwell,
because the boat
the shifty moon,
because the pollen
is a dusty glove
on tarmac, because
the crab is inside
out, because want
warmth, comfort
despair, hessian
and a smell of clay
in rain, because,
despite it all,
a pillow, despite
the streetlights

sleep, despite
the jackhammers
dawn, because
the night, because
the hell of appetite,
because the damp
sand on an empty
beach, because
a quickening, as if
that were enough,
is enough, because,
despite it all,
a lumbering sound,
an odor of fat
on the foggy air,
smoke, the smell
of cows, of grass,
of prehistoric
ferns, because,
despite it all,
a moon like
a membrane, rubber
valve through which
the weather comes,
because the cold,
because the pull
of underearth,
because the endless
weather, because,
despite it all
despite it all
the weather.

Rocks

If this is all there is
then I can live with that
(time that is
and the way it goes too quick)
but if it is not,
if there is more
(and when they say more
they mean much more)
then I do not see
how one can own this fact,
that we come to the light
like rocks in a plot of land
and have no choice
and will not cease to be,
and live.

How it ends

It was the great wind down,
clocks' ghosts being given up,
the beginning of the end.

At first it was barely discernible,
the noise of a plane on a windy night,
a roar a little denser than the hum;
and then when it was unmistakable,
it was as if it had always been there,
and that was the middle of the end.

Two for one

Life is not, nor has it ever been, what it
used to be, but a forward-leaning heap
of stuff; you scoot around in a collective
past for patterns and end up with what?
Stereotypes at best, a mishmash of like-
lihoods and clichés masquerading as rules
to choose your actions by. I stopped into
The Cock at Smithfield for one last pint
before the market closed; I was down
for the day on what I'd been given,
nothing major but down all the same.
Whittle, whittle – it's not so much
the money, more a question of potential.
You start with something and accrete
as you go along until you're pretty big,
like a dungball, and say, *hell, I'm going
to start giving off*; then before you know
it you're tiny again if you haven't
had the discipline to hoard a little too.
And not just a little either; my friend
in Normandy with the thousand bottle
cellar buys two for every one he drinks.
Two for every one. I hailed a cab,
stopped the driver when the meter
said '15' and walked. I was feeling
groggy but good, and bed could wait.

I admire

the ones
like Michelangelo
who make it
to old age
despite
the struggle

It seems
so easy
to fall off the edge
where the job
of its nature
will have
you work

that those who don't
are paradise
to me,
a safe
soft
place
like you
in
bed
forever

Those who stop
or whose
lives
are punctured

by
silence
I avoid

and the shimmering
early promise
come
to nought
turn
against
like tribes
do albinos

sunday

sunday
afternoon filled
our house, charcoal
coloured and form
less like an
unlicked
bear
but
we
were
in
it,
all
of
us,
so
best
to
make
of
it
what
we
could
taken in order
the day's minutes stack
taken as a whole
stack like an onion

'Yes sunday' ran the text, meaning
an afternoon filled with rearranging
your house, charcoal sketches make
discoloured and formal rooms look
a bit less like an asylum, cover that
pale sunlicked patch on the silk rug,
make it bearable at least, they drink
nothing but fruit juice, eat anything,
a sunflower swivelling with motion
solar-powered and also solar-aimed
is fulfilling perfect appetite perfectly, thus it, not omnivorous, unfussy
'oh it's all fine by me' houseguests
who proof read juice packaging but
not menus, is who you want to stay,
you are sort of reconciled, grousing
freely's best to calm nerves, decide
to drive to town and get some films
(slick remakes of Bogart and Bacall
the sort of thing they would be into)
so any bitterness after supper about
exactly what was said will not have
time, however hard it tries, to erupt
(or else could just pretend you were
mistaken in order to avoid dispute);
but the day's minutes stack up, and
are taken as a whole, you pass by a
haystack like an onion and see that.

Cathedral

All that porphyry to say suffering
is not for nothing, that there is no death.
Last night music came up through the shower
from the bar next door; then, this morning, rain.

there were all these birds
purnam adah purnam idam

there were all these birds, I couldn't tell you how many
in the fifty foot mess of ivy and wisteria
we'd let grow up our and the neighbours' wall,
and twice a day the birds, sparrows mainly,
some wood pigeon and a pair of blackbirds
who had three, then two, then three young again
all in the space of one spring
into summer, in the time it takes
for a human child
                to move
from lying to sitting eight birds
from one couple
                grew and left
the nest,
        and every time the parents
flew in to feed them
                  and every time
the young
        batted their wings
against that vegetal wall
in the week or so
                it took them
to fly
    and above all
                every time
those countless sparrows
went in and out and in and out
shaking down the dead leaves
                      trapped

God knows how long
                        behind the living ones
so that twice a day
                despite it being
spring and summer
                    the ground
would be covered in brown leaves,
                                twigs
and dried guano
            that tangle
of plants   would loosen
unnoticeably,   unnoticeable
until the night
what must have been tonnes
of water fell and under the weight
of that water and under its own weight
the growth peeled off from the wall
and folded, birds and all, and fell bent
double like an omelette in our yard

for a day after we cleaned it up
                            the birds,
instead of heading away,
          kept returning
to the spots on the wall
their perches had been, and then,
instead of heading
                away,
they all of them crowded
into the one remaining clump
of wisteria that, growing up tight
against the house, had weathered

the rainstorm,
                all those numberless
birds, used to
moving in a leafy
acre,
        squeezed
in this corner
                as if
even a fragment
                of what was home
is preferable
                to home
elsewhere
as if
    the quivering
thing inside
will keep
coming back
so long
as something,
no matter
how small
or torn,
remains

Nowhere special

The slightest movement
sets the iron bed
shaking; I know less
now than I used to,
less and less each day;
like just this morning
there was a dead man
in the underground
and I did nothing,
didn't even cross
myself; what's the point;
I just kept walking
with all the other
folk and by the time
I'd figured it out
was the other side
of the barrier;
oh there is blessing
to be haggled for,
sure, but not by me;
I try not to aim
anywhere as such,
head nowhere special;
I've got this idea
I keep to myself
that if I stay still,
I mean really still
so that the trembling
stops, I'll uncouple
hope from desire;

it's just an idea,
I can't guarantee
anything, but that
would be something, no?

2007

The city's filled with seagulls, foxes, spores.
Our winter clothes will be museum pieces;
then the water will cover our museums.

Letter from Iceland

I. Earthquake

Peace, the sun, a whimbrel on the grass
and under this the thing that nags
and shakes the house, and makes you write:
Peace, the sun, a whimbrel.

II. Hot tub

I'm sitting in the hot tub in the rain and the rain
is coming down sideways
so my chest and face are getting cold
while my fundament heats from underneath
like
one
of
those
long
thin
things
in
deep
sea
vents
that mine a difference in heat for life;
it seems that that there is and not that there is not
is down, in no small part, to them
so I open a beer and sit in the hot tub in the rain.

III. Keldur

I don't understand anything: why I came into
this body, this life;
my wife says I think too much,
that I have too much free time,
but I wouldn't want less, and besides,
I'd hardly call it free.
Up the road there is what was a house
and now is a building on a farm;
before the house there was nothing,
and around the farm there is nothing still.

IV. The monks

Like sperm come too late to an egg the monks
arrived in their coracles, wriggled, prayed
on the coast a while, then passed; they left no trace.

V. Sanctity

You put out to sea and nine times in ten
it's suicide; otherwise sanctity.

The point of pain

The normal example
  is hammering your thumb
or grabbing a burning
  pot, but what about pain
so great it's out of whack
  with self-preservation?
Fainting from a stubbed toe,
  a bollock-knock ending
you like tilted pinball,
  migraine, panic attacks
all argue a larger
  economy of pain
where hurt is rehearsal
  and remembered rooms stop
adults dead in their tracks.

I went down in the basement

I went down in the basement to speak to God, my id.
It was dank and irrational and God said *What*
do you want from me? I said *Truth*
or peace, a sign, anything, even the smallest thing,
and he showed me limbs, a tangle of body parts. *Why*, he said,
when you pray do you pray to pain?
Because it is irrefutable, I replied, *and vast, and I cannot fathom it.*
And what do you ask of it? To leave me be.

I went outside to a white sun in a grey sky,
and a woman sat on the lawn and sang.

Static

In half-lit rooms a radio tuned to nothing buzzes static,
a burr like the music of history,

which explains nothing
but without which we cannot explain;

it is this sound not silence we wake and sleep to
and by it know we are the same that wake who slept.

Ariel out of synch with the sun

He'd rather he hadn't written his poems:
too many eggs for not enough omelette.
But then who else would have? The sun
has been absent a while now leaving
questions whose answers are themselves
poems, and no vital reason to ask them.

Stately

We wouldn't advise it, not now the light
is stretched like the skin on a boy's ribs;
best wait until things thicken up;
the mistake beginners make
is to try and get out
too early, panic
pure and simple;
understandable
when you think of what's there
in the hadal depths: polyps,
membranes, merest smudges of life
but in such numbers that when they rise
all the measurable sea is solid,
fifty million species julienned
and not with the sharpest of knives
so that among the minnows
and translucent bean sprouts,
larger objects bob,
awkward wedges
that approximate
too well to memory,
the way at all times a choice
is forming between the moment
and the optimum repartition
in light of what you hope to have achieved;
which is why we advise our clients
to think of their holiday plans
and the like before rushing
willy-nilly to fix
time like a whale
makes ambergris;
on most projections
this is the middle sea,
leaving you free to explore
or float as you see fit, stately
an adjective perfectly suited
to both kinds of Portuguese man-of-war.

Ball bearings

There is a thing in pigeons freeze
and shake them they rattle sometimes
I think a similar lode must be in me
the size and shape of a neonates fist
it buffets and sucks me all over
the shop one year with nothing
better to do I noted my movements
on a chart and ignoring anomalies
found four and twenty principal
homes tweed then leather sometimes
country sometimes town from time
to time the doglike lamp post urge
betters me or a laughing man says
Gemaldegalerie and I melt we call this
lump in beasts magnetite in me soul.

Theories of Justice

It was after glue had been poured on the town
then lifted off like a gummy negative
that the folk went naked through the naked streets
to test the persistence of law in a world
where daylight showed no tact or history,
their shoulder blades, haunches and genital scraps
advancing in silence past the sandstone walls.

Well, here I am

Well, here I am with all of my love
  and all of my anger
            and all my mistakes

a heavy boat manoeuvres up the Schelde,
and the wind slams shut the bedroom door

a little inland, pollen in clouds
shifts like a dynasty
            moves over land

& I have no landscape
            save the landscape

within
  my mind   its better eye

lighting our house like sun in Hong Kong smog;

my kids, like the creature,
            resent their birth

they will hold it against existence forever
a slanting house in an orderly terrace

       and all ingenuity
          turned towards war

to the putting asunder of what was once one;

a gust of wind blows open the window
and then slams shut the bedroom door.

by the sea

the burning sand
like glass is damp
and silver: grape
flesh; sticky fists
of pine; a tortoise
necked like sex
clips succulents

by the sea

    the burning sand
    like glass is damp
    and silver

                    at night dry eyes: a mouth
  of grape flesh;

green-veined moisture

                    eucalyptus   juniper

          sticky fists of pine

  rabbits and hoopoes

              move across
                          the lawn; at dawn

      a tortoise
necked like sex
clips succulents

by the sea

    silver

                                    eyes: a mouth

    grape flesh;

green-veined moisture

                eucalyptus

        hoopoe

       ex

clips

by the sea

    ver

                                      yes
      esh;

                        calyp

lip

Miłosz in California

We are more than just meat he whispered
to the swimmers at the beach,
but the swimmers mistook his whispering for the wind
and looked for the white foam lifting from the waves.

We are more than just meat he said,
but the swimmers heard *eat*,
came out of the water
and shared out fruit among them.

We are more than just meat he bellowed
from his hill above the sea,
but the swimmers had left and the black waves
laved then uncovered the beach,
and swimmers, waves and beach,
nothing bellowed back.

May

It came in dreams like the day upstairs
on the bus commentary from a tourist
bus came in the window and all
of us were like nuclei or vanilla
flecks in ice cream;
                         the same thing
given like corned beef to a cargo cult
to everyone to chug away down
the pollinating summer street
with and do with what they will.

Much

Because
little
is true
beyond
its own
terms we
assume
nothing
can be
surely
known so
that that
selfsame
nothing
becomes
both end
(that is
failing)
and end
(that is
summum)
of thought;
but since
little
exists
outside
its own
terms this
selfsame
nothing

is not
only
only
sometimes
true but
also
when it
is is

More

Try
and
not
let
one
bad
one
put
you
off
or
if
it
is
to
be
so
so
be
it,
ill
can
cloud
light
like
that
time
when
life
went

grey
hope
fled
far
and
all
you
had
was
weight;
when
that
fell
from
your
back
like
snow
fall
from
roof
tops
the
day
was
big;
yes
one
bad
one
had
put
you

off
and
one
and
one
and
one
had
hid
you
yet
your
self
held
warm
and
one
and
all

Figs

The city is cold but somewhere figs
swell in an October sun.

Today the huge idea of money stopped
but the force which makes money gather and burst,
which used to move through God
and some say will again,
will outlive money itself.

Because things are
they have a preference for life,
and we call good whatever lets them grow.

Acknowledgements

Some of these poems have appeared in: *Alba, Anemone Sidecar, Barrow Street, Blackbox Manifold, cancan, DIAGRAM, Ekleksographia, Eyewear, Great Works, Greying Ghost Pamphlet Series, The London Magazine, NO/ON, Nthposition, PFS Post, Retort Magazine, Shadowtrain, The Stinging Fly, Tears in the Fence* and *Versal;* the anthologies *The Reiver's Stone* (Ettrick Forest Press, 2010), *11 9/ Web Streaming Poetry* (AUROPOLIS, 2010) and *Lung Jazz* (Cinnamon Press/Eyewear, 2012); and the chapbooks *Make Nothing Happen* (Oystercatcher Press, 2009) and *Liquiddity* (Oystercatcher Press, 2011).

EYEWEAR PUBLISHING

EYEWEAR POETRY
MORGAN HARLOW MIDWEST RITUAL BURNING
KATE NOAKES CAPE TOWN
RICHARD LAMBERT NIGHT JOURNEY
SIMON JARVIS EIGHTEEN POEMS
ELSPETH SMITH DANGEROUS CAKES
CALEB KLACES BOTTLED AIR
GEORGE ELLIOTT CLARKE ILLICIT SONNETS
HANS VAN DE WAARSENBURG THE PAST IS NEVER DEAD
DAVID SHOOK OUR OBSIDIAN TONGUES
BARBARA MARSH TO THE BONEYARD
MARIELA GRIFFOR THE PSYCHIATRIST
DON SHARE UNION
SHEILA HILLIER HOTEL MOONMILK
FLOYD SKLOOT CLOSE READING
PENNY BOXALL SHIP OF THE LINE
MANDY KAHN MATH, HEAVEN, TIME
MARION McCREADY TREE LANGUAGE
RUFO QUINTAVALLE WEATHER DERIVATIVES
SJ FOWLER THE ROTTWEILER'S GUIDE TO THE DOG OWNER
TEDI LÓPEZ MILLS DEATH ON RUA AUGUSTA

EYEWEAR PROSE
SUMIA SUKKAR THE BOY FROM ALEPPO WHO PAINTED THE WAR